199

For Ellie
D.C.

To Marko
D.K.

This edition published by Parragon in 2013

Parragon Inc.
440 Park Avenue South, 13th Floor
New York, NY 10016
www.parragon.com

Published by arrangement with Gullane Children's Books
185 Fleet Street, London, EC4A 2HS

Text © David Conway 2008
Illustrations © Dubravka Kolanovic 2008

ISBN 978-1-4723-2431-3

Printed in China

...we love you

David Conway

illustrated by

Dubravka Kolanovic

PaRragon

Bath • New York • Singapore • Hong Kong • Cologne • Delhi
Melbourne • Amsterdam • Johannesburg • Shenzhen

One night, while the whole house was sleeping, the toys in the playroom discovered an old abandoned bear that the children had found. Its fur was matted and its ears were worn. It looked like the most bedraggled and unhappy teddy bear that ever was.

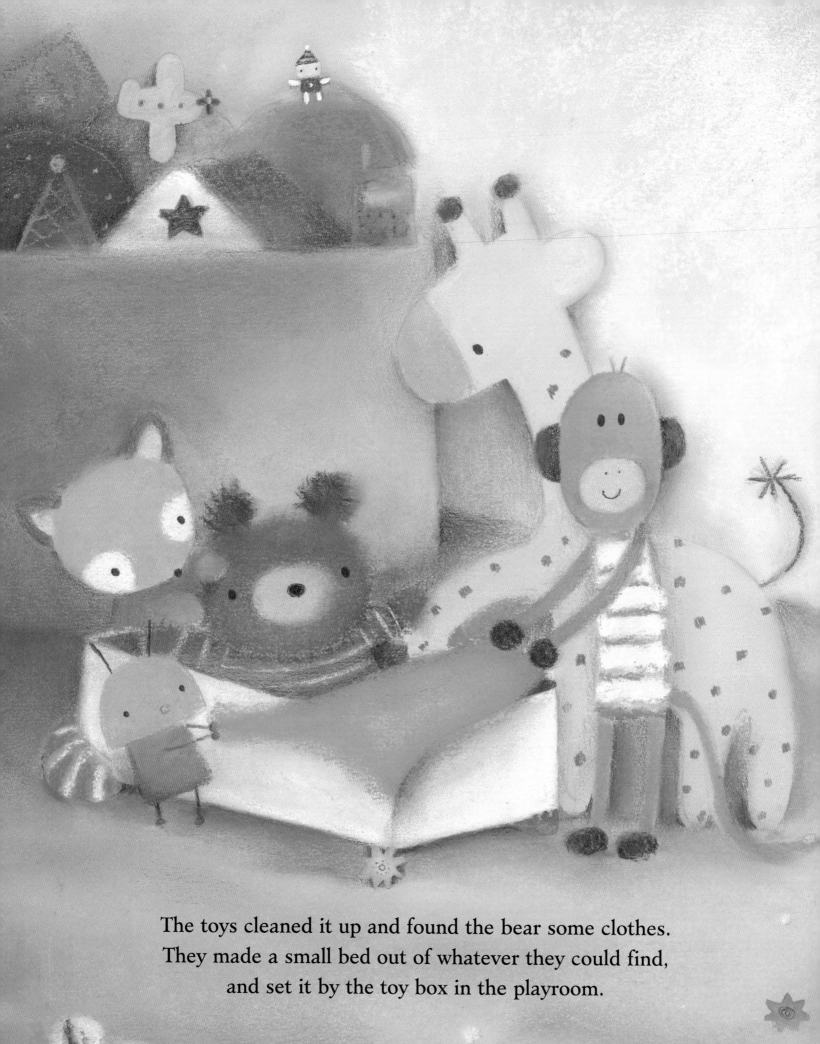

The toys cleaned it up and found the bear some clothes.
They made a small bed out of whatever they could find,
and set it by the toy box in the playroom.

But despite all their efforts there was a problem. The shabby
old bear seemed just as sad as when they had found it.
"It's his heart," said the giraffe, "it's broken. That bear
needs more than clothes and a comfortable bed
to sleep in. It needs to feel happy again."

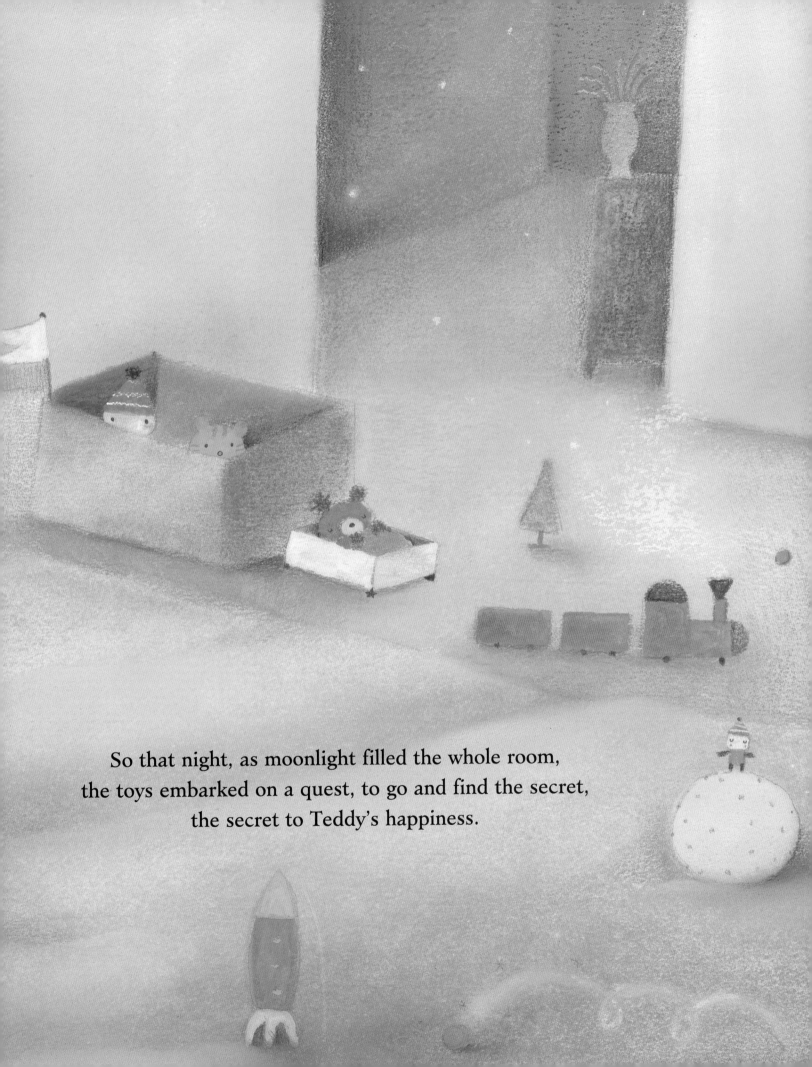

So that night, as moonlight filled the whole room,
the toys embarked on a quest, to go and find the secret,
the secret to Teddy's happiness.

They rode a train,

and then a plane . . .

and sailed on a carpet sea.

They searched the playroom and rummaged around.
But they could not find the secret. No secret could be found.

Then the friends encountered a rabbit who
knew everything there was to know, from the
height of the tallest building, to where
the snow goes when it's not winter.

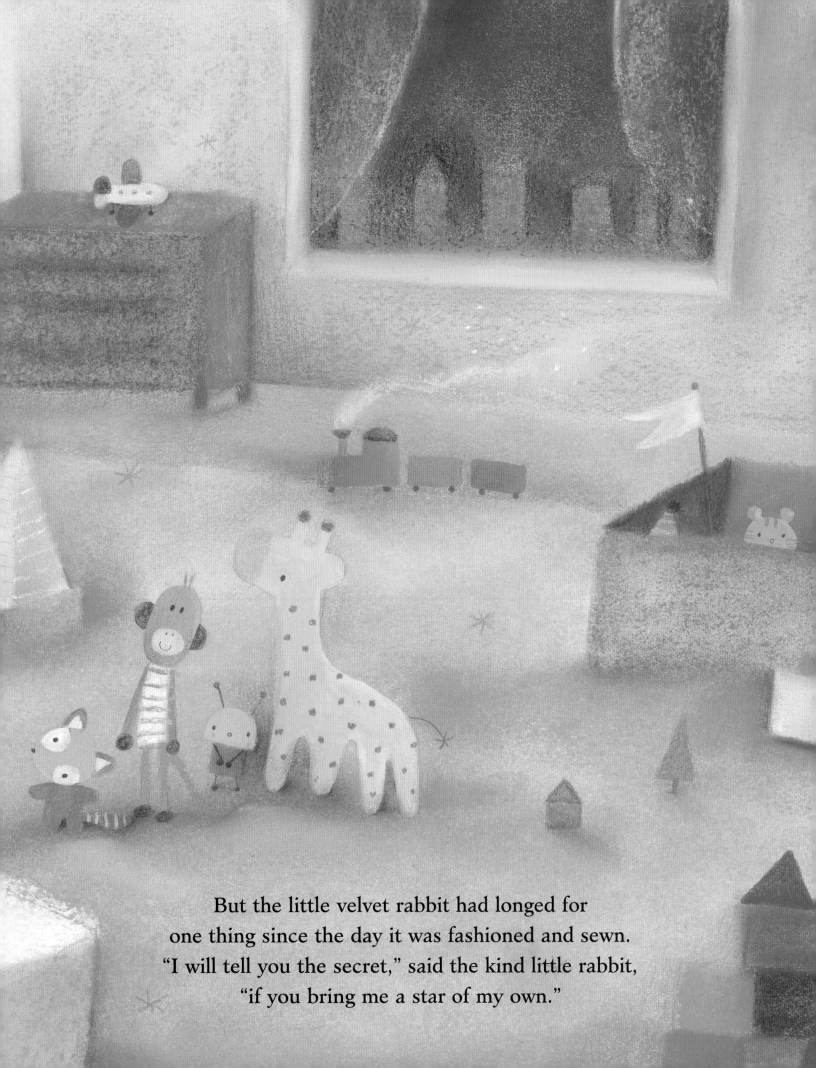

But the little velvet rabbit had longed for
one thing since the day it was fashioned and sewn.
"I will tell you the secret," said the kind little rabbit,
"if you bring me a star of my own."

So the adventurous toys went in
search of a star in a rickety old toy car.

They found some hanging in the baby's room,
attached by strings to a luminous moon.
"I will give you a star," whispered the moon, "but then,
you must shine a light upon me so I can glimmer again."

So the brave little toys went in search of a light
as all the clocks in the house struck midnight . . .

They found one on an island by a shabby
old lion, but the lion wanted something in return.

"It is cold on this island," said the sleepy old lion, in a
slow and slumberous yawn. "But I will give you this light
if you bring me a scarf that will keep me nice and warm."

So the monkey, the robot,
the raccoon and the giraffe
set off in the moonlight
to search for a scarf . . .

along the dark,
murky hallway . . .

down a mountain steep . . .

where they found one piled up
with some coats in a heap.

Then the party of friends returned to the island
and wrapped the scarf around the lion's mane . . .

they cast the light upon the luminous
moon to make it glow and glimmer again . . .

they flew to the bookshelf on a rocket ship
where the little velvet rabbit lived all alone . . .

and presented it with a tiny star,
one it could call its own.

Then the rabbit revealed the secret
and with an air of cheerfulness,
uttered three tiny words into
the shadowy gloom—
the secret to Teddy's happiness.

So they rode a train . . .

then a plane . . .

and sailed the whole night through,
with three tiny words for a sad old bear,
three magical words . . .

...we love you.